Thomas Nelson and Sons Ltd
Nelson House Mayfield Road
Walton-on-Thames Surrey
KT12 5PL UK

51 York Place
Edinburgh
EH1 3JD UK

Thomas Nelson (Hong Kong) Ltd
Toppan Building 10/F
22A Westlands Road
Quarry Bay Hong Kong

Thomas Nelson Australia
102 Dodds Street
South Melbourne
Victoria 3205
Australia

Nelson Canada
1120 Birchmount·Road
Scarborough Ontario
M1K 5G4   Canada

© Templar Publishing Ltd 1985
First published by Hamlyn Publishing 1985
Second and subsequent impressions published by Thomas Nelson & Sons Ltd from 1989

Letterland was devised by Lyn Wendon and is part of
the *Pictogram* system © Lyn Wendon 1973-1986

ISBN 0-17-410159-7
NPN 9876

Printed in Italy

Annie Apple's Adventure

Written by Vivien Stone

Illustrated by
Jane Launchbury

Collins

An imprint of HarperCollins*Publishers*

One afternoon an astronaut landed in Letterland. He didn't mean to come to Letterland. He arrived by accident.

"I wonder where I am?" he said as he climbed out of his spaceship.

He looked around him at all the trees. Then he heard a small voice.

"This is Letterland," said the voice. "Can I help you?"

The astronaut looked up into a tree close by. There he saw a round red apple hanging from a branch. For a moment he thought he was dreaming. Or did the apple really have a happy smile on its face?

The voice came again.
"My name is Annie Apple,"
it said. "Who are you?"

The astronaut was astonished.
"I'm called Alan," he said.
"I didn't mean to land here.
I had a little trouble with my spaceship."

"Oh dear," said Annie. "Wait, I think
I know someone who can help.
If you lift me off this branch I will take
you to him."

Again the astronaut was amazed.
He had never met such a helpful apple
before.

He lifted Annie Apple down from her
branch and together they set off across
Letterland.

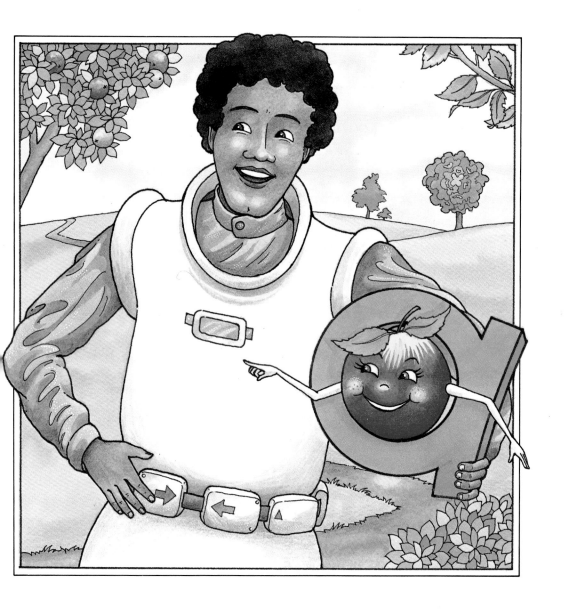

"I'm taking you to meet my friend Ticking Tom," said Annie Apple. "He knows nearly everything."

Soon they came to Ticking Tom's Tower. Annie explained how the astronaut had arrived in Letterland by accident. Then Alan explained what had gone wrong.

"My radio went pop suddenly," he said, "so I couldn't ask anyone where I was – or where I was going."

"I think I can help," said Tom. He started to collect all kinds of tools together.

Back at the spaceship Ticking Tom and the astronaut set to work immediately. Soon they had the radio in little pieces.

"Here's the trouble," said Tom holding up a wire that was still smoking. "Too many amps!"

In no time at all the radio was fixed and Alan was talking to his friends out in space. Finally, he turned to Annie and Tom.

"They said I've got to test the radio up in space," he said. "They want you both to come with me, in case anything goes wrong again."

Annie beamed. "What an adventure!" she said.

Even Ticking Tom had never been in a spaceship before. He and Annie sat in their seats and fastened their seat belts.

Alan started his count down. "FIVE, FOUR, THREE, TWO, ONE, LIFT OFF!" The spaceship shot up like an arrow.

Annie felt squashed in her seat. She looked round at Tom. His face looked very strange. "Don't worry about the squashed feeling," said Alan. "It's just the G-force as we accelerate."

Annie Apple didn't know what that meant. "Accelerate means going faster and faster," said Ticking Tom.

Soon Annie's adventure became even more exciting. They were up in space and orbiting the Earth. Round and round they went.

Inside the spaceship Annie and Tom undid their seat belts.

They both started to float away from their seats.

They were having great fun turning somersaults.

"I feel like an acrobat!" cried Annie happily.

At the window of the spaceship they could look down on the Earth. It looked very small and a long way away.

"Look, there's the Atlantic Ocean," said Ticking Tom.

"And there's Letterland," said Alan the Astronaut, pointing at a little blob on the Earth.

"I can't see any apples," said Annie.

"That's because you are so far away," said Ticking Tom with a smile.

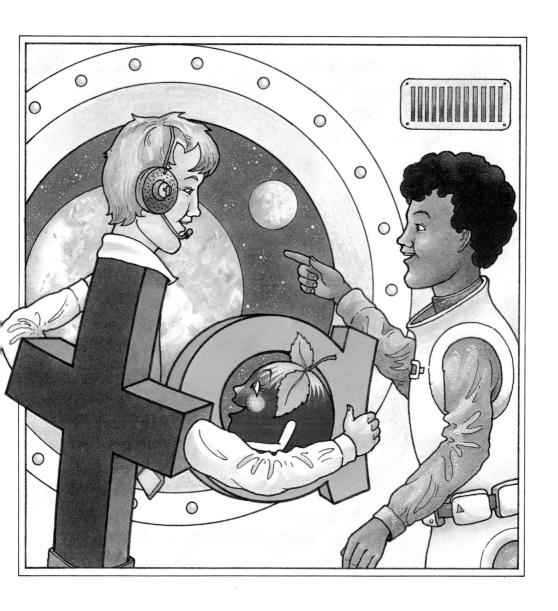

Then something strange started to happen. While Alan was testing his radio again, and Ticking Tom was looking at Letterland through a telescope, Annie Apple was changing shape!

Instead of a round apple, she was beginning to look more like a long thin apple. In fact, she was becoming more and more sausage-shaped!

Annie shrieked. Now she was becoming as flat as a pancake!

"I think Annie has had enough of being in space," said Alan.
"It must be the weightlessness!"

"Time to go back to Letterland," said Tom.

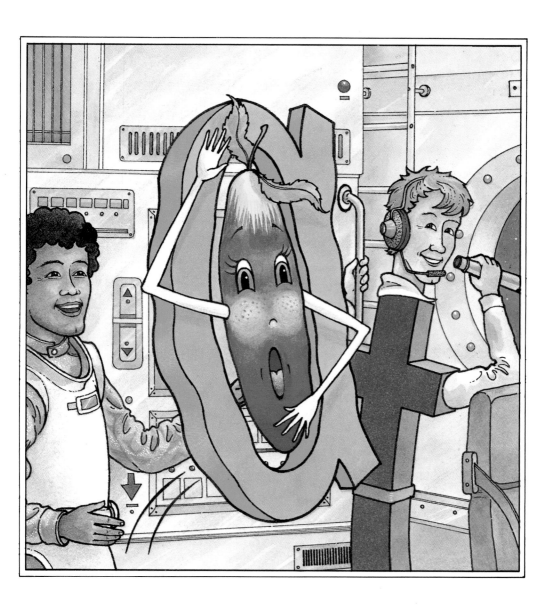

Soon the spaceship was racing back to Earth. It hardly seemed to take a moment.

Annie Apple still looked a bit strange as she sat in her seat, but she was slowly returning to her normal shape.

Now she looked a bit fatter and rounder.

"I still feel like a pancake!" she said grinning at Tom.

"You won't for long," replied Tom. "We are about to arrive in Letterland again. Then you will feel better."

The spaceship finally came back to Earth and Annie Apple felt much better. She also looked apple-shaped again.

"What a relief," said Alan. "I'm glad you're all right."

"It was a real adventure," said Annie. "I hope you can come again."

For a moment Alan looked sad. "I have to travel a long way from here and I don't think I can find my way back."

Now it was Annie's turn to look sad, but not for long. Suddenly she disappeared into Ticking Tom's tower.

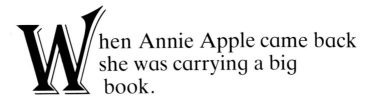

When Annie Apple came back she was carrying a big book.

"This will help you find your way back to Letterland," she cried happily. "It's the Letterland Atlas! It shows you where EVERYWHERE is!"

Alan the Astronaut smiled. "That will be useful," he said. "Thank you very much."

"Now you can come to see us again," said Annie Apple, "and next time, not by accident!"

THE END